JUV/E
FIC

Sharmat, Marjorie
Weinman.

I'm the best!

$14.95

R0086330182

DATE			
AUG 5 1991			

I'M THE BEST!

by Marjorie Weinman Sharmat

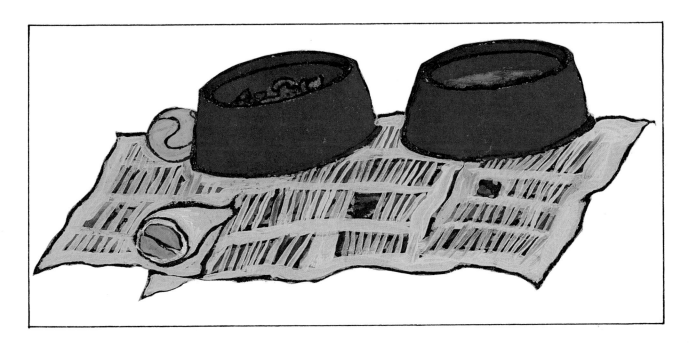

illustrated by Will Hillenbrand

Holiday House / New York

Library of Congress Cataloging-in-Publication Data

Sharmat, Marjorie Weinman.
I'm the best! / by Marjorie Weinman Sharmat ;
illustrated by Will Hillenbrand.—1st ed.
p.   cm.
Summary: A dog who has lived with many owners
and many different names finally finds
the family that wants to keep him
and love him forever.
ISBN 0-8234-0859-0
[1. Dogs—Fiction.] I. Hillenbrand, Will, ill. II. Title.
PZ7.S5299Ip 1991   90-39176   CIP   AC
[E]—dc20

For my husband Mitch, who gave me the idea for this book, and for our Fritz and our Dudley, who inspired it

M.W.S.

For my wife Jane, with a special thank you to Pat and Michael Randolph, who are members of one of Dudley's families.

W.H.

My name is Dudley, but once I was named Sparky. Before that I was Fluffy. For two months I was Mopsy. I think I was Cedric for a week. I've had a lot of names.

And owners. Some of them liked me. Some of them didn't. My first owner gave me away when I ate his plant.

My second owners gave me away when they moved to Pennsylvania.

My third owner died.
After that I lost count of my owners.

I remember the last one. She named me Dudley. She got me a silver tag with my name on it.

But she gave me to the Humane Society when she decided to take a trip around the world.

I wanted to go with her.

Now here I am, waiting for a new person.

Or family. I keep telling myself, "I'm the best, but nobody knows it yet."

Look at them looking me over. Listen to what they're saying.

"Too much fur."
"Do you like his tail?"
"I don't trust his eyes."
"A shedder."
"Maybe . . ."
"No!"

Then I hear, "Oh look, isn't he cute! He looks so much like Fritz, Mom."

"Maybe that's not good, Robert."

"It's good, Dad."

"His card says his name is Dudley. He seems gentle."

Gentle? Is that an insult?

I bark.

"His bark sounds a little like Fritz's used to, Mom."

Now I hear the words I've heard before:
"I want him! We'll take him."
They *want* me!
But for how long?
My new family signs papers. Now I have a boy and his
mother and father.

We get into their car and drive home. They have a nice house. I know houses. I know apartments. I know farms. I know condos. I've lived in all of them.

They take me into the kitchen. On the floor I see a bowl of food. And a bowl of water. Both bowls have a name on them: FRITZ.

Oh well. Food's food. Water's water. After I eat, the boy says, "You'll sleep in my room." And he takes me there.

"How do you like our room, Fritz?"
Fritz? The name's Dudley, remember? Who is Fritz?
The boy hugs me. I wag my tail at him.

"I'm Robert," he says.
I bet he's only had one name in his whole life. He crawls
into bed. He doesn't invite me in. Oh, well. The floor's my
place, anyway. ZZZZZZZzzzzzzz.

The next morning, Robert says, "Time for breakfast."

We go to the kitchen. One bowl that says FRITZ is full of kibbles. The other bowl that says FRITZ is full of water.

I eat and drink while Robert and his mother and father eat muffins and drink orange juice.

"You look perky today, Fritz," Robert's mother says.

I AM NOT FRITZ! I came with a silver tag. It says DUDLEY on it.

"His name's Dudley," Robert's father says.

He remembers. Good sign.

"I miss Fritz," Robert says.

"We had him for over fourteen years," Robert's mother says. "Even before you were born, Robert."

Oh, I get it.

Fritz was their dog. He got old, I guess. And that was that. They really miss him. Too bad. Sad.

"But, listen folks," I want to yell. "I can't take anybody else's place. I'm just me . . . Sparky, Fluffy, Mopsy, Cedric, Dudley."

"I'm going to take him for a walk and show him to my
friends," Robert says.

I love walks. I absolutely *love* walks. Robert gets a
leash. We're off.

"Want to run, Fritz?" he asks.

Yeah, away from home. Maybe they'll miss me, Dudley.

"Fritz ran away from home nine times," Robert says.
"He always came back."

Running away won't impress them. They'll just wait
until I come back.

Or maybe they won't care.

Now three weeks have gone by. I've been called Fritz seventy-eight times. People think dogs can't count, but nobody ever proved it.

Well, the food's good. Robert's good and full of hugs. His mother and father are kind.

I ate one of their plants this morning.

They don't care about the plant.

But they're worried that it could make me sick.

They take me to the vet's.

Dr. Burton has me up on a table. She's poking and looking and hmmmmm-ing.

"Dudley's fine," she says. "The plant he ate was harmless."

She knows my name. Maybe I'll go live with her.

"I think Dudley likes plants," she says.

"You'll have to break the habit," she tells me.

Sometimes you can't break habits. I eat plants. They call me Fritz.

Now I've been here five weeks.
I've picked a special place to sleep on Robert's bed.
They've given me my own sock to chew on.

And they've bought me a plastic hot dog and bun to play with. We play toss and run and fetch.

They toss. I run and fetch.

Robert takes me for lots of walks and runs. Sometimes his mother does too. And his father.

The pats are endless. And I get brushed once a day. I think they are somewhere between liking me and loving me.

They're keeping me. Forever. At last I'm being kept forever. They called me Dudley four times this week. At last they're catching on. But who cares?

Not me . . . Sparky, Fluffy, Mopsy, Cedric, Dudley and Fritz.

Whoever I am, I'm home.